HAPPY
Birthday
imagination

Happy birthday, Puffin!

Did you know that in 1940 the very first Puffin story book (about a man with broomstick arms called Worzel Gummidge) was published? That's 70 years ago! Since then the little Puffin logo has become one of the most recognized book brands in the world and Puffin has established its place in the hearts of millions.

And in 2010 we are celebrating 70 spectacular years of Puffin and its books! Pocket Money Puffins is a brand-new collection from your favourite authors at a pocket-money price – in a perfect pocket size. We hope you enjoy these exciting stories and we hope you'll join us in celebrating the very best books for children. We may be 70 years old (sounds ancient, doesn't it?) but Puffin has never been so lively and fun.

There really IS a Puffin book for everyone
– discover yours today.

Books by Sarah Dessen

Sarah Dessen

Infinity

PUFFIN

PUFFIN BOOKS

Published by the Penguin Group
Penguin Books Ltd, 80 Strand, London WC2R ORL, England
Penguin Group (USA) Inc., 375 Hudson Street, New York, New York 10014, USA
Penguin Group (Canada), 90 Eglinton Avenue East, Suite 700, Toronto, Ontario, Canada M4P 2Y3
(a division of Pearson Penguin Canada Inc.)
Penguin Ireland, 25 St Stephen's Green, Dublin 2, Ireland (a division of Penguin Books Ltd)
Penguin Group (Australia), 250 Camberwell Road, Camberwell, Victoria 3124, Australia
(a division of Pearson Australia Group Pty Ltd)
Penguin Books India Pvt Ltd, 11 Community Centre, Panchsheel Park, New Delhi – 110 017, India
Penguin Group (NZ), 67 Apollo Drive, Rosedale, North Shore 0632, New Zealand
(a division of Pearson New Zealand Ltd)
Penguin Books (South Africa) (Pty) Ltd, 24 Sturdee Avenue, Rosebank,
Johannesburg 2196, South Africa

Penguin Books Ltd, Registered Offices: 80 Strand, London WC2R ORL, England

puffinbooks.com

'Infinity' first published in the USA in *SIXTEEN: Stories About That Sweet and Bitter Birthday*
by Three Rivers Press (imprint of The Crown Publishing Group) in 2004
Just Listen first published in the USA by Viking, a member of Penguin Group (USA), Inc. 2006
First published in Great Britain by Penguin Books 2007
That Summer first published in the USA by Orchard Books, 1996
First published in Great Britain by Penguin Books 2009
Published in this edition 2010

1

Text copyright © Sarah Dessen, 2010
Colour Puffin artwork on cover copyright © Jill McDonald, 1974
All rights reserved

The moral right of the author and illustrator has been asserted

Set in Adobe Caslon 11.75/19pt
Typeset by Ellipsis Books Limited, Glasgow
Made and printed in England by Clays Ltd, St Ives plc

Except in the United States of America, this book is sold subject to the
condition that it shall not, by way of trade or otherwise, be lent, re-sold, hired out,
or otherwise circulated without the publisher's prior consent in any form of binding
or cover other than that in which it is published and without a similar condition
including this condition being imposed on the subsequent purchaser

British Library Cataloguing in Publication Data
A CIP catalogue record for this book is available from the British Library

ISBN: 978-0-141-33077-8

www.greenpenguin.co.uk

Mixed Sources
Product group from well-managed
forests and other controlled sources
www.fsc.org Cert no. SA-COC-1592
© 1996 Forest Stewardship Council

Penguin Books is committed to a sustainable future
for our business, our readers and our planet.
The book in your hands is made from paper
certified by the Forest Stewardship Council.

Contents

Infinity

Lately, I don't dream about Anthony. I dream about the roundabout.

Now, Mr Haskell, my psychology teacher, would say this had implications. That somehow my fear of the roundabout is linked to my issues with Anthony, which are both many and complicated. Mr Haskell has a certain way he says things like this, leaning over with both elbows balanced on his lectern. It's very unsettling, as if he can see deep into your soul. But the truth is I was scared of the roundabout before I even met Anthony.

Most towns have those most modern of inventions, traffic lights, to deal with traffic. Not here. Instead, some genius decided however many years ago to put in instead this big circle with all the main roads feeding into it, then sat back to watch people crash to their deaths as they attempted to negotiate it.

But I digress.

My first experience with the roundabout was when I was about seven. We'd just moved to town so that my father could finally finish his dissertation. My mother and I were on our way to the grocery store when we suddenly came up on this big sign that said YIELD with an arrow pointing to the right. Cars were going round a big circle, off which poked several different exits to different roads. The trick, apparently, was to kind of merge in, follow round until your exit, then merge out. Simple as that.

'Oh, my God,' my mother said, poking her glasses

up the bridge of her nose, which she always does when she's really nervous. 'What is this?'

The answer came in the form of a loud, impatient beep from behind us. My mother looked anxiously to her left, then tentatively tapped at the accelerator, sending us inching out into oncoming traffic. Another beep.

'Mom,' I said.

'I'm merging!' she shrieked, as if this was on the level of splitting atoms and I was distracting her on purpose. And we were merging, pretty well, slowly easing into traffic. In fact, we were almost relaxed when we had to try and get back out, no easy trick, as there were many cars merging in. We got stuck on the inside track for two more turns, watching our exit go by, before my mother panicked and just sort of jerked the wheel, sending us in its general direction. And that was when the station wagon hit us.

The scene ensued the way you would expect: dents all around, tears (my mother), angry muttering (the guy who owned the station wagon), plus everyone else driving past rubbernecking and jawing to each other while I sank down as far as I could in the passenger seat, wishing there was a way to meld permanently with the pleather beneath me. The entire episode ended with a ticket, our insurance rates rising and my mother swearing to never do the roundabout ever again, which seemed somewhat overly dramatic, until we realized that she meant it.

What this means, essentially, is that she has spent nine years taking the longest possible route *everywhere*, because the roundabout is the hub of our town. Avoiding it takes work. And maps. And no end of secret shortcuts, long detours and general embarrassment. Even a trip to the Quik Zip, basically about four miles from our house, requires getting on the highway, cutting (illegally) through the senior-citizen compound and three left turns against oncoming traffic.

My father calls this ridiculous. He is a roundabout

champ, folding easily in and out, even while chatting on his cell phone or fiddling with the CD player. He is also a mathematician, something that my mother always brings up whenever the Roundabout Argument commences, as if his proficiency with numbers is somehow involved in his mastery of the traffic circle. What all this has meant to me is that when it comes to going anywhere I'm usually hoping it's my dad who grabs the keys to the sedan off the hook by the door first. Which is going to be a moot point, now that I'm about to turn sixteen and get my own licence.

My boyfriend, Anthony, is a year older than me. He's good at the roundabout too, but understands my hesitation. In fact, since I got my permit, we've spent a lot of time going in circles together, practising. We started late at night, when it was pretty much deserted.

'Okay, now the first thing you're gonna do is stop and look to the left here,' he instructed me one night.

'There's someone coming, so unless they merge off before they get here, we'll wait for them to pass.'

We waited. It was a Cadillac, moving slowly. They had the whole roundabout to themselves.

'Okay now,' Anthony said. 'Just ease out.'

I did. Just as my mother had, all those years ago. But this time there was no one coming; it was dark. No problem. But still my heart was beating hard, thumping against my chest, even as I picked up speed.

'See?' Anthony said, reaching over to squeeze my leg. He left his hand there, warm on my skin, as we eased round the circle. 'Piece of cake, right?'

'Right,' I said. We passed all the exits once, then started through again. Of course this was okay, I thought. Like a merry-go-round, only faster. But it was a trial run. And trial runs are always easier.

After a few more turns we were starting to get dizzy. Finally Anthony pointed towards the beach route exit, and I took it, following the bumpy road past subdivisions and marshes before finally hitting the turn-off to the shore parking lot. I slowed down, remembering the potholes, pulling up into a space right behind the lifeguard stand. Then I cut the engine.

'You did good tonight,' Anthony said.

'Thanks,' I said.

And then he leaned over and kissed me. I knew he would. I knew it just like I knew after a few minutes he'd reach up and undo my shirt, then slide off my bra straps, easing me back against the seat behind me. He'd tell me he loved me, kiss my neck, run his hand down my back and into the waistband of my jeans, pressing his fingers there. I knew because we'd been practising this too, all this time, trial run after trial run. Like the roundabout, what came next was obvious. And scary. And, it seemed, inevitable.

I'd been with Anthony for over six months. We'd met at work: we both had jobs at Jumbo Smoothie. He worked the blenders, which was an advanced position, while I dumped sliced peaches and yoghurt into cups, prepping. It wasn't a great job, but we got to play the radio and eat all the free smoothies we wanted, which was fun for the first week or so.

Anthony was tall, with a bony frame: he had big wrists, wild curly hair and a sloping kind of walk that always made him look like he was taking his time. When he blended smoothies, he really put his whole body into it, arms shaking, bouncing on the balls of his feet, like the noise the blender made was music and he just couldn't help himself from dancing.

He wanted to sleep with me. He hadn't come out and said it, but he didn't really have to. He was a senior; we'd been together six months. Us having sex would be a natural progression, after kissing to letting him go up my shirt, then down my jeans: like moving from learner's permit to licence, there's only one thing left. And so I have this choice. To either merge in or take the long way home.

'I'm so proud of you!'

That was my mother when I came out of the

DMV office, holding my new licence. It was still warm in my hand from where they'd laminated it, as if it was somehow alive.

'Let me see the picture,' she said. She squinted down at it. 'Very nice. You're not even blinking.'

It was a decent shot. I'd even had a second to brush my hair while the guy was arguing with some woman over her picture – she'd blinked, I guess – which I figured was a bonus. And there, next to my face, was all my pertinent information. Height, weight, eye colour. Birthday. And expiry date: 2014. Amazing. Where would I be in four years?

'McDonald's,' my mother said when I asked her this. We were in the car. I was driving.

'What?' I said.

'I thought we should go to McDonald's,' she said. She fiddled with her sun visor, up then down. Although she'd never admit it, my mother was nervous riding with me. 'To celebrate.'

'Oh,' I said. 'Okay.'

McDonald's was smack in the middle of the lunch rush, the noise of registers and commotion and the crackling of the drive-through speaker almost over-powering. My mother told me to go find a table, then stood in line clutching her purse. The people behind her were all public-works guys in orange jumpsuits, talking too loudly.

I found a table by the window and sat down. The surface was covered with salt, like a dusting of snow, too thin to see but you could feel it. I moved my finger through it, leaving a circle behind, until suddenly someone put their hands over my eyes.

'Guess who?' a voice said right next to my ear. It was Anthony. Without my sight, the McDonald's seemed to get quieter, as if you needed to see all the commotion for it to really be happening.

'I know it's you,' I said softly, reaching up and putting my hands over his. I could feel the silver ring he wore on his index finger pressing gently against my eyelid, cool and smooth. He went to move his hands, the joke being over, but I kept them there for a second longer before he slipped loose and it was bright again.

'So, did you get it?' he asked, dropping one hand on to my neck and leaning over me. I reached into my pocket and pulled out my licence, showing him. 'Nice. Good picture too. You're not even blinking or making a weird face.'

'Nope,' I said. Anthony's licence picture was terrible. Just when the guy was about to pop the flash someone slammed a door, and Anthony was startled: in the picture he looks surprised, like his eyes are bugging out of his head. But it doesn't bother him. He says no one really looks like their licence picture anyway. 'I'm lucky, I guess.'

'Yes,' he said, curving his hand round the back of my neck the way that always gave me chills. 'You are.'

'Well, hello there!' My mother set the tray down in front of me. Two chicken sandwiches with no mayo, two large fries, two Diet Cokes. We both always get the same thing. 'Are you joining us?'

Anthony reached over, took one of my fries and popped it into his mouth. 'Nope,' he said. 'Some of us have to get back to school.'

'Poor you,' I said, taking my fries off the tray.

'I'll call you later,' he said, bending down again and kissing my cheek in a very chaste, little-sister kind of way. Normally I would have at least got it on the lips, but my mother was right there. Still, she ducked her head and pretended to be very busy opening ketchup packets until he walked away, waving once over his shoulder. 'Get ready for that roundabout!' he called out, and then the glass doors swung shut behind him.

My mother picked up her sandwich, adjusting the one piece of lettuce and one tomato: they never give you enough, and the distribution is always all wrong. 'You know,' she said finally, taking her first bite, 'you don't have to do the roundabout right away.'

'I know,' I said. We'd already discussed this during the weeks I'd had my permit, when she'd officially taught me all of her extended shortcuts. 'But I think I should just go ahead and get it over with.'

She took a sip of her drink and glanced out of the window. We'd both known this day was coming, eventually. My mother and I were close, always had been. She didn't fall into any of the specific Mom types: she wasn't Nagging Mom, or Trying-To-Be-Young-And-Hip-Mom, or Super-Strict Mom. My parents were rumpled academics. Books had been their greatest love, before me, and I just knew that when I had flown the nest and was long gone they'd continue their set patterns, floating from the break-fast nook, which had the best morning light, to the big couch by the fireplace, where they could each take an armrest with their stacks of journals and novels between them. Sentences and paragraphs, themes and symbols, these were things my mother never feared. She had a Ph.D and did *The New York*

Times crossword every morning before she even had her first cup of coffee. Words didn't scare her, only shapes. Like circles.

She'd expected me to fall in with this. I knew it by the way she'd easily assumed I'd learn her shortcuts, memorizing them so that I, too, could take a four-mile circuitous route to the post office that was, measured by the clean numbers of my odometer, a mere half mile away. My father had harrumphed at this, my mother's lessons in avoidance, and hinted broadly that maybe my induction into the driving public would be a good excuse for my mother to finally face this, the fear of all fears. But I, for one, doubted this would ever happen. My mother had got accustomed to taking the long way everywhere: it wasn't even a burden for her any more. That's the thing about habits. And fears. At first they might seem like trouble, but eventually they just fold in, becoming part of the fabric, a jumped stitch you hardly notice except when someone else points it out.

Now, watching her sip her drink, I felt a tug of obligation. She was the lone roundabout holdout, and wasn't it my duty, as her daughter, to stand with her in allegiance? On the other side was not only the rest of our town, but more importantly my father, fearless warrior of traffic circles, and Anthony, who had crashed his parents' Volvo once on a roundabout one town over and still not thought twice about going back for more. I longed for the simple, solid logic of traffic lights, no decisions necessary: green means go, red means stop, yellow means slow down or run the light, make up your mind though because time's a-wasting. All straight lines, or variations thereof.

Out in the parking lot, my mother and I buckled up and I backed out slowly, careful of the cars lining up for the drive-through. 'Good turning,' she said, praising my slow but effective merging into traffic on the main road. She had her hands in her lap, fingers locked, and we didn't talk as we moved through three intersections, catching the green light at each. Up ahead I could see the signs for the round-about, warning us of its approach. My mother pulled her fingers tighter, like a Chinese puzzle, and looked out of the window quickly, as if the office-supply store on her right was suddenly fascinating.

I could do this. It wasn't any different to all those nights I'd merged and circled the roundabout with Anthony or my father: the traffic was just a little heavier. I was not the bravest of girls, but I'd never been branded a coward either. I told myself I wasn't just doing this for me, but for my mother as well. I pictured us breezing easily round the curves, the weight of this burden suddenly lifting, my achieve-ment sparking something in her as well, just as my father had hinted. The traffic was picking up now, the last intersection coming up in front of us. The engine seemed to grind as I downshifted, the other drivers pressing in around me.

There was a honk a few cars back – not at us, but loud nonetheless – and I have to admit it threw me, sending a quick hot flush up the back of my neck. It didn't help, of course, that my mother gasped in a breath loud enough for me to hear over the wind whistling through my not-quite-shut window. And, just like that, I lost my confidence, my hand reaching up to hit the right turn signal as if it had made the choice all by itself. As we took the turn on to Murphey's Chapel Road, my mother loosened her fingers, pressing them against the fabric of her skirt. Puzzle solved.

'It's okay,' she said as we breezed past a few neigh-bourhoods, with only two left turns, one access road and a shopping-centre parking lot to traverse before home. 'You'll do it when you're ready.'

She was relieved. I could hear it in her voice, see it in the slow easing of her shoulders back against the headrest. But I was angry with myself for duck-ing out. It seemed a bad way to begin things, with a false start, a last-minute abort so close to take-off. As if I'd come this far, right to the brink, and in pulling back set a precedent that would echo, like the sound of my mother's gasp, next time.

I avoided the roundabout for a week and a half. There were several almosts, most of them with Anthony in the car, pep-talking me like a motivational coach.

'Be the road!' he urged me as we coasted up to the ROUNDABOUT AHEAD signs. He'd made mixed CDs, full of bouncy, you-can-do-anything kind of songs, which he blasted, thinking they were helping. Instead, they distracted me entirely, as if by failing to complete the task meant letting down not only myself and Anthony but several bands and singers from all over the world. 'Visualize it! Breathe through it!'

But, always, I took that last possible right turn. The music would play on, unaware of its ineffectiveness, while Anthony would just shake his head, easing an elbow out of the window, and say nothing.

His urging was gentler, but no less insistent,

when the car was off and we were alone together at the beach. There was music then, too, but it was softer, soothing, as was his voice, in my ear, or against my neck.

'I love you, I love you,' he'd whisper, and I'd feel that same hot flush, travelling up from my feet, the adrenalin rush that was a mix of fear and longing. We'd got very close, but again I pulled back. Scared. It seemed ludicrous that I was unable to follow through with anything, as if from sixteen on I was doomed to be ruled by indecision.

'I just don't understand why you don't want to,' he asked me one night as we sat looking at the water, him now leaning against his door, as far away from me as possible, as if the fact that I didn't want him made it necessary to put the maximum amount of distance between us. There was no grey here, no compromise. We'd come up so quickly on all or nothing that it blindsided me, a mere glint out of the corner of my eye before full impact.

'I want it to be right,' I told him.

'How can this not be right?' He sat up straighter, jutting a finger up at the windshield. 'Moonlight? Check. Crashing waves? Check. I love you? Check. You love me . . .'

It took me a second, just a second, to realize it was my turn to say something. 'Check,' I said quickly, but he glared at me and let his finger drop, as if this explained everything.

As the days passed, and I found myself consistently taking the long way to everything, I got frustrated with all these decisions. A part of me wanted to barrel into the roundabout blindfolded, pushing the accelerator hard, and let whatever was going to happen just happen, anything for it to be over. The same part sometimes was so close to giving in to Anthony's pleadings, wanting to finally just relax against the seat and let him do what he wanted, let his fingers spread across my skin, trailing downward, just give it all up and finally ease myself of these burdens. Scenario number one, of course, was stupid: I'd cause a multi-car pile-up and kill myself. As far as number two, well, it was harder to say. What would change? Maybe there wouldn't be visible damage, dented bumpers or crumpled hoods. But something in me would be different, even if no one else could tell. Like a car that's been wrecked and fixed, but the frame stays bent, and only the most trained of eyes can feel it pull on curves, or nudge towards the right on straight roads. Just because you don't see it doesn't mean something isn't there. Or gone.

The fall carnival appeared in one afternoon, with rides and sideshows and the huge Ferris wheel cropping up in a field by the shopping mall as if dropped from the sky itself. In daylight, as I took my short-cut to school, everything looked tired and rusted, the tarps covering equipment flapping, workers walking around with craggy faces, half asleep. But by that night, with the lights blazing and the sounds of the carnies rounding up business for the games, it was like a whole new world.

Anthony walked in, bought some cotton candy and proceeded to lose twenty bucks in about five minutes playing a game that involved shooting water pistols at stuffed frogs. I just stood and watched him, silent after my first three tries to point out he was never, ever going to win.

'Tough luck, buddy,' the guy running the game said in a monotone voice, his eyes on the crowd moving past, already looking for the next sucker.

'One more time,' Anthony said, digging out some more bills. 'I'm getting closer. I can feel it.'

'How badly do you really need a frog anyway?' I asked him. They looked like the typical carnival stuffed animals I remembered from my childhood, the kind with nubby fur that smelled faintly like paint stripper. They always looked better before you actually won them, as if the minute the carnie handed them over they faded, or diminished somehow, the golden ring gone brass.

'It's not about the frog,' Anthony snapped at me, bending down to better line up his shot. 'It's about winning.'

'Winning a frog,' I grumbled, but he just ignored me, then slammed his fist down and stalked off when he lost. Again. He cheered up a little bit when I used my money to buy cake and tickets for the Ferris wheel, then stood in line with me, chewing loudly, the frog forgotten.

Behind us was a guy with his daughter, who looked to be about eight. She had a big stuffed lion under her arm and was gripping her dad's hand, staring up at the Ferris wheel as it moved lazily above us.

'Now, honey,' the man said, squatting down beside her, 'you don't have to go on it if you don't want to.'

'I want to,' she said firmly, switching the lion to the other arm.

'Because it might be scary.'

'I want to,' she repeated.

'Okay,' he said, in the kind of voice that was usually accompanied by a shrug. As if he doubted this, her conviction. But as I watched her face, the careful way she studied the ride as it came to a stop, I envied her for knowing exactly what she wanted. But it was easy when you're little, I figured. Not so many choices.

We got on the ride, and as Anthony pulled the safety bar towards us I craned my neck round, watching to see if the little girl would get into the next seat. She did, without hesitation, planting her lion next to her and laying her hands in her lap, as if she was only getting on a bus, or sitting in a chair, the world to remain always solid beneath her.

As we started moving, Anthony wrapped both his hands round mine and kissed my neck. I closed my eyes as we moved up, higher and higher, our seat rocking slightly. The Ferris wheel was higher than I'd thought and, staring down, everything seemed to shrink to a pinpoint. I could see the steeple from the church on my corner in the distance, beyond that the lights from the football fields. From up high, everything seemed closer together than it actually was, as if the further away you got, the more the world you knew folded in to comfort itself.

Anthony was sliding his hands on to my stomach, moving one to the small of my back, one down my waistband, murmuring in my ear. We were still rising, higher and higher, and someone was screaming a few cars down, but I told myself it wasn't that little girl, not her. In my mind, I saw her solid face, her absolute determination, and refused to believe it would be so easy to sway her.

We were at the very top when I looked down and felt dizzy. Anthony was pressing against me, his fingers digging, hardly caring that this was not the place, not the time, so determined was he to win whatever it was he wanted so badly, that seemed so ideal, at least as long as it shrank back from his grasp. All those nights at the beach, when I'd pushed him away, I hadn't known exactly why, just that it hadn't felt right. But as my view from high up narrowed, I realized that my relationship with Anthony had done the same, going from a wide endless horizon of possibilities to one pinpoint of a destination. I wanted to have choices, to know that I could, at any moment, still take the long way home. Sure, there was a quick way to anywhere. But sometimes, when you took the shortcut, you missed the view.

'I love you,' he whispered in my ear. 'I want you.'

But it wasn't enough, this time. Maybe later it would have been, but as I pushed him away, I knew that time would never come. Winning might not have been everything, but Anthony was tired of losing at this game. If he couldn't have me, he'd find an easier prize.

The ride hadn't even come to a full stop when he pushed the safety bar away from us. It rattled, loudly, and sent a ripple of force through my metal seat, an echo I felt in my bones. Then he stomped down the stairs to the sideshows, pushing past all the people lined up for the next ride while I climbed out slowly, taking my time, telling myself to pay attention to how the earth felt beneath me and not take it for granted any more.

I'd driven, and Anthony was gone, lost in the crowd of sticky wrappers and screaming children and all the voices of the game workers, their coaxing and wheedling like a swarm of bees hovering. When I finally got to my car, it seemed like everyone was leaving at once, a long snaky trail of brake lights leading out to the main road.

I pulled up behind a pickup truck and then sat there, moving forward in tiny increments, watching the traffic light up ahead drop from red to green, then climb to red again. Even though I'd only been driving for a couple of weeks it already felt more natural. Things that before I'd had to think about consciously, like switching gears and working the clutch, now happened automatically, as if that part of my mind was handling it, making those decisions for me. Maybe that was all it took, in the end, was the time to let the new soak in. To stand in the face of change and size it up, acquaint yourself, before jumping in. It was all the pressure that was so hard, those little nudges forward, poke poke poke. If you just backed off, and let it come to you, it would.

When I finally made it to the light, I hit my indicator, signalling the left turn that would lead me around the shopping mall and through two neighbourhoods before depositing me neatly on to my own road. It was the way I'd always gone, up until now, but this time I didn't feel that burning burst of shame in it, knowing I was taking the easy way out. I just remembered the view from up high, the way all the roads led to each other eventually. It didn't matter which route you took, as long as you got home.

I was thinking this as I moved up to the solid green of the light. That burst of freedom in realizing that my choice was okay. But even so, at the last minute, I turned my wheel to the right, surprising even myself, and shifted into second as the roundabout came up into my sight. It was crowded with carnival traffic, cars whizzing past: I could see it, as if I was still up high, the absolute geometry of that perfect circle. This was normally the moment I was dumb scared, hands shaking, but this time I only pressed further, closer, pressing my shoulders back against the seat as if taking the scariest, and most exhilarating of rides.

As I got nearer, I glanced in my rear-view mirror, and saw the Ferris wheel. It was far behind me, brightly lit, and looked small enough to slide on my finger and keep there. Another circle, representing a kind of infinity that I was only beginning to understand. So when I looked back at the road, easing myself closer to the roundabout traffic, I sealed that image in my mind as I merged in, holding my breath, and felt myself fall into the rhythm of the cars around me. I turned the wheel, leaning into the first curve, feeling that rush of accomplishment and speed as we all moved away from the centre, further and further out. It was happening so fast, but I was there, right there, alive, wanting this moment to be like brass rings and Ferris wheels and all the circulars of this life and others, never ending.

Extract from
Just Listen

I taped the commercial back in April, before anything had happened, and promptly forgot about it. A few weeks ago, it had started running and, suddenly, I was everywhere.

On the rows of screens hanging over the ellipticals at the gym. On the monitor they have at the post office that's supposed to distract you from how long you've been waiting in line. And now here, on the TV in my room, as I sat at the edge of my bed, fingers clenched into my palms, trying to make myself get up and leave.

'It's that time of year again . . .'

I stared at myself on the screen as I was five months earlier, looking for any difference, some visible proof of what had happened to me. First, though, I was struck by the sheer oddness of seeing myself without benefit of a mirror or photograph. I had never got used to it, even after all this time.

'Football games,' I watched myself say. I was wearing a baby-blue cheerleader uniform, hair pulled back tight into a ponytail, and clutching a huge megaphone, the kind nobody ever used any more, emblazoned with a K.

'Study hall.' Cut to me in a serious plaid skirt and brown cropped sweater, which I remembered feeling itchy and so wrong to be wearing just as it was getting warm, finally.

'And, of course, social life.' I leaned in, staring at the me on-screen, now outfitted in jeans and a glittery tee and seated on a bench, turning to speak this line while a group of other girls chattered silently behind me.

The director, fresh-faced and just out of film school, had explained to me the concept of this, his creation. 'The girl who has everything,' he'd said, moving his hands in a tight, circular motion, as if that were all it took to encompass something so vast, not to mention vague. Clearly, it meant having a megaphone, some smarts and a big group of friends. Now, I might have dwelled on the explicit irony of this last one, but the on-screen me was already moving on.

'It's all happening this year,' I said. Now I was in a pink gown, a sash reading HOMECOMING QUEEN stretched across my midsection as a boy in a tux stepped up beside me, extending his arm. I took it, giving him a wide smile. He was a sophomore at the local university and mostly kept to himself at the shooting, although later, as I was leaving, he'd asked for my number. How had I forgotten that?

'The best times,' the me on-screen was saying now. 'The best memories. And you'll find the right clothes for them all at Kopf's Department Store.'

The camera moved in, closer, closer, until all you could see was my face, the rest dropping away. This had been before that night, before everything that had happened with Sophie, before this long, lonely summer of secrets and silence. I was a mess, but this girl – she was fine. You could tell in the way she stared out at me and the world so confidently as she opened her mouth to speak again.

'Make your new year the best one yet,' she said, and I felt my breath catch, anticipating the next line, the last line, the one that only this time was finally true. 'It's time to go back to school.'

The shot froze, the Kopf's logo appearing beneath me. In moments, it would switch to a frozen waffle commercial or the latest weather, this fifteen seconds folding seamlessly into another, but I didn't wait for that. Instead, I picked up the remote, turned myself off, and headed out of the door.

*

I'd had over three months to get ready to see Sophie. But when it happened, I still wasn't ready.

I was in the parking lot before first bell, trying to muster up what it would take to get out and officially let the year begin. As people streamed past, talking and laughing, en route to the courtyard, I kept working on all the maybes: maybe she was over it now. Maybe something else had happened over the summer to replace our little drama. Maybe it was never as bad as I thought it was. All of these were long shots, but still possibilities.

I sat there until the very last moment before finally drawing the keys out of the ignition. When I reached for the door handle, turning to my window, she was right there.

For a second, we just stared at each other, and I instantly noticed the changes in her: her dark curly hair was shorter, her earrings new. She was skinnier, if that were possible, and had done away with the thick eyeliner she'd taken to wearing the previous spring, replacing it with a more natural look, all bronzes and pinks. I wondered, in her first glance, what was different in me.

Just as I thought this, Sophie opened her perfect mouth, narrowed her eyes at me and delivered the verdict I'd spent my summer waiting for.

'Bitch.'

The glass between us didn't muffle the sound or the reaction of the people passing by. I saw a girl from my English class the year before narrow her eyes, while another girl, a stranger, laughed out loud.

Sophie, though, remained expressionless as she turned her back, hiking her bag over one shoulder and starting down to the courtyard. My face was flushed, and I could feel people staring. I wasn't ready for this, but then I probably never would be, and this year, like so much else, wouldn't wait. I had no choice but to get out of my car, with everyone watching, and begin it in earnest, alone. So I did.

*

I had first met Sophie four years earlier, at the beginning of the summer after sixth grade. I was at the neighbourhood pool, standing in the snack-bar line with two damp dollar bills to buy a Coke, when I felt someone step up behind me. I turned my head, and there was this girl, a total stranger, standing there in a skimpy orange bikini and matching thick platform flip-flops. She had olive skin and thick, curly dark hair pulled up into a high ponytail, and was wearing black sunglasses and a bored, impatient expression. In our neighbourhood, where everyone knew everyone, it was like she'd fallen out of the sky. I didn't mean to stare. But, apparently, I was.

'What?' she said to me. I could see myself reflected in the lenses of her glasses, small and out of perspective. 'What are you looking at?'

I felt my face flush, as it did any time anybody raised their voice at me. I was entirely too sensitive to tone, so much so that even TV court shows could get me upset – I always had to change the channel when the judge ripped into anyone. 'Nothing,' I said, and turned back round.

A moment later, the high-school guy working the snack bar waved me up with a tired look. While he poured my drink I could feel the girl behind me, her presence like a weight, as I smoothed my two bills out flat on the glass beneath my fingers, concentrating on getting out every single crease. After I paid, I walked away, studiously keeping my eyes on the pocked cement of the walkway as I made my way back round the deep end to where my best friend, Clarke Reynolds, was waiting.

'Whitney said to tell you she's going home,' she said, blowing her nose as I carefully put the Coke on the pavement beside my chair. 'I told her we could walk.'

'Okay,' I said. My sister Whitney had just got her licence, which meant that she had to drive me places. Getting home, however, remained my own responsibility, whether from the pool, which was walking distance, or the mall one town over, which wasn't. Whitney was a loner, even then. Any space around her was her personal space; just by existing, you were encroaching.

It was only after I sat down that I finally allowed myself to look again at the girl with the orange bikini. She had left the snack bar and was standing across the pool from us, her towel over one arm, a drink in her other hand, surveying the layout of benches and beach chairs.

'Here,' Clarke said, handing over the deck of cards she was holding. 'It's your deal.'

Clarke had been my best friend since we were six years old. There were tons of kids in our neighbourhood, but for some reason most of them were in their teens, like my sisters, or four and below, a result of the baby boom a couple of years previously. When Clarke's family moved from Washington, D.C., our moms met at a community-watch meeting. As soon as they realized we were the same age, they put us together, and we'd stayed that way ever since.

Clarke had been born in China, and the Reynoldses had adopted her when she was six months old. We were the same height, but that was about all we had in common. I was blonde-haired and blue-eyed, a typical Greene, while she had the darkest, shiniest hair I'd ever seen and eyes so brown they were almost black. While I was timid and too eager to please, Clarke was more serious, her tone, personality and appearance all measured and thoughtful. I'd been modelling since before I could even remember, following my sisters before me; Clarke was a total tomboy, the best soccer player on our block, not to mention a whiz at cards, especially gin rummy, at which she'd been beating me all summer.

'Can I have a sip of your drink?' Clarke asked me. Then she sneezed. 'It's hot out here.'

I nodded, reaching down to get it for her. Clarke

had bad allergies year-round, but in summer they hit fever pitch. She was usually either stuffed up, dripping, or blowing from April to October, and no amount of shots or pills seemed to work. I'd long ago grown used to her adenoidal voice, as well as the omnipresent pack of Kleenex in her pocket or hand.

There was an organized hierarchy to the seating at our pool: the lifeguards got the picnic tables near the snack bar, while the moms and little kids stuck by the shallow end and the baby (i.e., pee) pool. Clarke and I preferred the half shaded area behind the kiddie slides, while the more popular high-school guys – like Chris Pennington, three years older than me and hands-down the most gorgeous guy in our neighbourhood and, I thought then, possibly the world – hung out by the high dive. The prime spot was the stretch of chairs between the snack bar and lap lane, which was usually taken by the most popular high-school girls. This was where my oldest sister, Kirsten, was stretched out in a chaise, wearing a hot-pink bikini and fanning herself with a *Glamour* magazine.

Once I dealt out our cards, I was surprised to see the girl in orange walk over to where Kirsten was sitting, taking the chair next to her. Molly Clayton, Kirsten's best friend, who was on her other side, nudged her, then nodded at the girl. Kirsten looked up and over, then shrugged and lay back down, throwing her arm over her face.

'Annabel?' Clarke had already picked up her cards and was impatient to start beating me. 'It's your draw.'

'Oh,' I said, turning back to face her. 'Right.'

The next afternoon, the girl was back, this time in a silver bathing suit. When I got there, she was already set up in the same chair my sister had been in the day before, her towel spread out, bottled water beside her, magazine in her lap. Clarke was at a tennis lesson, so I was alone when Kirsten and her friends arrived about an hour later. They came in loud as always, their shoes thwacking down the pavement. When they reached their usual spot and saw the girl sitting there, they slowed, then looked at one another. Molly Clayton looked annoyed, but Kirsten just moved about four chairs down and set up camp as always.

For the next few days, I watched as the new girl kept up her stubborn efforts to infiltrate my sister's group. What began as just taking a chair escalated, by day three, to following them to the snack bar. The next afternoon, she got in the water seconds after they did, staying just about a foot down the wall as they bobbed and talked, splashing one another. By the weekend, she was trailing behind them constantly, a living shadow.

It had to be annoying. I'd seen Molly shoot her a couple of nasty looks, and even Kirsten had asked her to back up, please, when she'd got a little too close in the deep end. But the girl didn't seem to care. If anything, she just stepped up her efforts more, as if it didn't matter what they were saying as long as they were talking to her, period.

'So,' my mother said one night at dinner, 'I heard a new family's moved in to the Daughtrys' house, over on Sycamore.'

'The Daughtrys moved?' my father asked.

My mother nodded. 'Back in June. To Toledo. Remember?'

My father thought for a second. 'Right,' he said finally, nodding. 'Toledo.'

'I also heard,' my mom continued, passing the bowl of pasta she was holding to Whitney, who immediately passed it on to me, 'that they have a daughter your age, Annabel. I think I saw her the other day when I was over at Margie's.'

'Really,' I said.

She nodded. 'She has dark hair, a bit taller than you. Maybe you've seen her around the neighbourhood.'

I thought for a second. 'I don't know –'

'That's who that is!' Kirsten said suddenly. She put down her fork with a clank. 'The stalker from the pool. Oh my God, I *knew* she had to be way younger than us.'

'Hold on.' Now my father was paying attention. 'There's a stalker at the pool?'

'I *hope* not,' my mother said, in her worried voice.

'She's not a stalker, really,' Kirsten said. 'She's just this girl who's been hanging around us. It's so creepy. She, like, sits beside us, and follows us around, and doesn't talk, and she's always listening to what we're saying. I've told her to get lost, but she just ignores me. God! I can't believe she's only *twelve*. That makes it even sicker.'

'So dramatic,' Whitney muttered, spearing a piece of lettuce with her fork.

She was right, of course. Kirsten was our resident drama queen. Her emotions were always at full throttle, as was her mouth; she never stopped talking, even if she were well aware you weren't listening to her. In contrast, Whitney was the silent type, which meant the few words she uttered always carried that much more meaning.

'Kirsten,' my mother said now, 'be nice.'

'Mom, I've tried that. But, if you saw her, you'd understand. It's strange.'

My mother took a sip of her wine. 'Moving to a new place is difficult, you know. Maybe she doesn't know how to make friends –'

'She obviously doesn't,' Kirsten told her.

'– which means that it might be your job to meet her halfway,' my mother finished.

'She's *twelve*,' Kirsten said, as if this was on par with being diseased, or on fire.

'So is your sister,' my father pointed out.

Kirsten picked up her fork and pointed it at him. 'Exactly,' she said.

Beside me, Whitney snorted. But my mom, of course, was already turning her attention on me.

'Well, Annabel,' she said, 'maybe you could make an effort, if you do see her. To say hello or something.'

I didn't tell my mother I'd already met this new girl, mostly because she would have been horrified she'd been so rude to me. Not that this would have changed her expectations for my behaviour. My mother was famously polite, and expected the same of us, regardless of the circumstances. Our whole lives were supposed to be the high road. 'Okay,' I said. 'Maybe I will.'

'Good girl,' she said. And that, I hoped, was that.

The next afternoon, though, when Clarke and I got to the pool, Kirsten was already there, lying out with Molly on one side and the new girl on the other. I tried to ignore this as we got settled in our spot, but eventually I glanced over to see Kirsten watching me. When she got up a moment later, shooting me a look, then headed towards the snack bar, the new girl immediately following her, I knew what I had to do.

'I'll back in a second,' I told Clarke, who was reading a Stephen King novel and blowing her nose.

'Okay,' she said.

I got up, then started round by the high dive, crossing my arms over my chest as I passed Chris Pennington. He was lying on a beach chair, a towel over his eyes, while a couple of his buddies wrestled on the pool deck. Now, instead of sneaking glances at him – which, other than swimming and getting beaten at cards, was my main activity at the pool that summer – I'd get bitched out again, all because my mother was insistent we be raised as the best of Good Samaritans. Great.

I could have told Kirsten about my previous run-in with this girl, but I knew better. Unlike me, she did not shy away from confrontation – if anything, she sped towards it, before overtaking it completely. She was the family powder keg, and I had lost track of the number of times I'd stood off to the side, cringing and blushing, while she made her various displeasures clear to salespeople, other drivers or various ex-boyfriends. I loved her, but the truth was, she made me nervous.

Whitney, in contrast, was a silent fumer. She'd never tell you when she was mad. You just knew, by the expression on her face, the steely narrowing of her eyes, the heavy, enunciated sighs that could be so belittling that words, any words, seemed preferable to them. When she and Kirsten fought which, with two years between them, was fairly often – it always seemed at first like a one-sided argument, since all you could hear was Kirsten endlessly listing accusations and slights. Pay more attention, though, and you'd notice Whitney's stony, heavy silences, as well as the rebuttals she offered, few as they were, that always cut to the point much more harshly than Kirsten's swirling, whirly commentaries.

One open, one closed. It was no wonder that the first image that came to mind when I thought of either of my sisters was a door. With Kirsten, it was the front one to our house, through which she was always coming in or out, usually in mid-sentence, a gaggle of friends trailing behind her. Whitney's was the one to her bedroom, which she preferred to keep shut between her and the rest of us, always.

As for me, I fell somewhere between my sisters and their strong personalities, the very personification of the vast grey area that separated them. I was not bold and outspoken, or silent and calculating. I had no idea how anyone would describe me, or what would come to mind at the sound of my name. I was just Annabel.

My mother, conflict-averse herself, hated it when my sisters fought. 'Why can't you just be *nice*?' she'd plead with them. They might have rolled their eyes, but a message sank in with me: that being nice was the ideal, the one place where people didn't get loud or so quiet they could scare you. If you could just be nice, then you wouldn't have to worry about arguments at all. But being nice wasn't as easy as it seemed, especially when the rest of the world could be so mean.

By the time I got to the snack bar, Kirsten had disappeared (of course), but the girl was still there, waiting for the guy behind the counter to ring up her candy bar. *Oh well*, I thought, as I walked up to her. *Here goes nothing*.

'Hi,' I said. She just looked at me, her expression unreadable. 'Um, I'm Annabel. You just moved here, right?'

She didn't say anything for what seemed like a really long while, during which time Kirsten walked out of the ladies' room behind her. She stopped when she saw us talking.

'I,' I continued, now even more uncomfortable, 'I, um, think we're in the same grade.'

The girl reached up, pushing her sunglasses further up her nose. 'So?' she said, in that same sharp, snide voice as the first time she'd addressed me.

'I just thought,' I said, 'that since, you know, we're the same age, you might want to hang out. Or something.'

Another pause. Then the girl said, as if clarifying, 'You want me to hang out. With you.'

She made it sound so ridiculous I immediately began backtracking. 'I mean, you don't have to,' I told her. 'It was just –'

'No,' she cut me off flatly. Then she tilted her head back and laughed. 'No *way*.'

The thing is, if it had just been me there, that would have been it. I would have turned round, face flushed, and gone back to Clarke, game over. But it wasn't just me.

'Hold on,' Kirsten said, her voice loud. 'What did you just say?'

The girl turned round. When she saw my sister, her eyes widened. 'What?' she said, and I couldn't help but notice how different this, the first word she'd ever said to me, sounded as she said it now.

'I said,' Kirsten repeated, her own voice sharp, 'what did you just say to her?'

Uh-oh, I thought.

'Nothing,' the girl replied. 'I just –'

'That's my sister,' Kirsten said, pointing at me, 'and you were just a total bitch to her.'

By this point, I was already both cringing and blushing. Kirsten, however, put her hand on her hip, which meant she was just getting started.

'I wasn't a bitch,' the girl said, taking off her sunglasses. 'I only –'

'You were, and you know it,' Kirsten said, cutting her off. 'So you can stop denying it. And stop following me around too, okay? You're creeping me out. Come on, Annabel.'

I was frozen to the spot, just looking at the girl's face. Without her sunglasses, her expression stricken, she suddenly *looked* twelve, just staring at us as Kirsten grabbed my wrist, tugging me back to where she and her friends were sitting.

'Unbelievable,' she kept saying, and, as I looked across the pool, I could see Clarke watching me, confused, as Kirsten pulled me down onto her chair. Molly sat up, blinking, reaching up to catch the untied straps of her bikini.

'What happened?' she asked, and, as Kirsten began to tell her, I glanced back towards the snack bar, but the girl was gone. Then I saw her, through the fence behind me, walking across the parking lot, barefoot, her head ducked down. She'd left all her stuff on the chair beside me – a towel, her shoes, a bag with a magazine and wallet, a pink hairbrush. I kept waiting for her to realize this and turn back for it. She didn't.

Her things stayed there all afternoon: after I'd gone back to sit with Clarke, and told her everything. After we played several hands of rummy, and swam until our fingers were pruny. After Kirsten and Molly left, and other people took their chairs. All the way up until the lifeguard finally blew the whistle, announcing closing time, and Clarke and I packed up and walked round the edge of the pool, sunburned and hungry and ready to go home.

I knew this girl was not my problem. She'd been mean to me, twice, and therefore was not deserving of my pity or help. But, as we passed the chair, Clarke stopped. 'We can't just leave it,' she said, bending over to gather up the shoes and stuff them into the bag. 'And it's on our way home.'

I could have argued the point, but then I thought again of her walking across the parking lot, barefoot, alone. So I pulled the towel off the chair, folding it over my own. 'Yeah,' I said. 'Okay.'

Still, when we got to the Daughtrys' old house, I was relieved to see all the windows were dark and there was no car in the driveway, so we could just leave the girl's stuff and be done with it. But, as Clarke bent down to stick the bag against the front door, it opened, and there she was.

She had on cutoff shorts and a red T-shirt, her hair pulled back in a ponytail. No sunglasses. No high-heeled sandals. When she saw us, her face flushed.

'Hi,' Clarke said, after a just-long-enough-to-be-noticed awkward silence. Then she sneezed before adding, 'We brought your stuff.'

The girl just looked at her for a second, as if she didn't understand what she was saying. Which, with Clarke's congestion, she probably didn't. I leaned over and picked up the bag, holding it out to her. 'You left this,' I said.

She looked at the bag, then up at me, her expression guarded. 'Oh,' she said, reaching for it. 'Thanks.'

Behind us, a bunch of kids coasted past on their bikes, their voices loud as they called out to one another. Then it was quiet again.

'Honey?' I heard a voice call out from the end of the dark hallway behind her. 'Is someone there?'

'It's okay,' she said over her shoulder. Then she stepped forward, shutting the door behind her, and came out onto the porch. She quickly moved past us, but not before I saw that her eyes were red and swollen – she'd been crying. And suddenly, like so many other times, I heard my mother's voice in my head: *Moving to a new place is tough. Maybe she doesn't know how to make friends.*

'Look,' I said, 'about what happened. My sister –'

'It's fine,' she said, cutting me off. 'I'm fine.' But, as she said it, her voice cracked, just slightly, and she turned her back to us, putting a hand to her mouth. I just stood there, totally unsure what to do but, as I looked at Clarke, I saw she was already digging into the pocket of her shorts to pull out her ever-present pack of Kleenex. She drew one out, then reached round the girl, offering it to her. A second later, the girl took it, silently, and pressed it to her face.

'I'm Clarke,' Clarke said. 'And this is Annabel.'

In the years to come, it would be this moment

that I always came back to. Me and Clarke, in the summer after our sixth-grade year, standing there behind that girl's turned back. So much might have been different for me, for all of us, if something else had happened right then. At the time, though, it was like so many other moments, fleeting and unimportant, as she turned round, now not crying – surprisingly composed, actually – to face us.

'Hi,' she said. 'I'm Sophie.'

Extract from
That Summer

It's funny how one summer can change everything. It must be something about the heat and the smell of chlorine, fresh-cut grass and honeysuckle, asphalt sizzling after late-day thunderstorms, the steam rising while everything drips around it. Something about long, lazy days and whirring air conditioners and bright plastic flip-flops from the pharmacy thwacking down the street. Something about fall being so close, another year, another Christmas, another beginning. So much in one summer, stirring up like the storms that crest at the end of each day, blowing out all the heat and dirt to leave everything gasping and cool. Everyone can reach back to one summer

*and lay a finger on it, finding the exact point when
everything changed. That summer was mine.*

The day my father got remarried, my mother was up
at 6 a.m. defrosting the refrigerator. I woke to the
sound of her hacking away and the occasional thud
as a huge slab of ice crashed. My mother was an
erratic defroster. When I came down into the kitchen,
she was poised in front of the open freezer, wielding
the ice pick, Barry Manilow crooning out at her from
the tape player she kept on the kitchen table. Around
Barry's voice, stacked in dripping piles, were all of
our perishables, sweating in the heat of another
summer morning.

'Oh, good morning, Haven.' She turned when she
saw me, wiping her brow with the ice pick still in
hand, making my heart jump as I imagined it slipping
just a bit and taking out her eye. I knew that nervous
feeling so well, even at fifteen, that spilling un-
controllability that my mother brought out in me. It

was as if I were attached to her with a tether, her every movement yanking at me, my own hands reaching to shield her from the dangers of her waving arms.

'Good morning.' I pulled out a chair and sat down next to a stack of packaged chicken. 'Are you okay?'

'Me?' She was back on the job now, scraping. 'I'm fine. Are you hungry?'

'Not really.' I pulled my legs up to my chest, pressing hard to fold myself into the smallest size possible. It seemed like every morning I woke up taller, my skin having stretched in the night while I slept. I had dreams of not being able to fit through doors, of becoming gigantic, towering over people and buildings like a monster, causing terror in the streets. I'd put on four inches since April, and showed no signs of letting up. I was already five eleven, with only a few more little lines on the measuring stick before six feet.

'Haven.' My mother looked at me. 'Please don't

sit that way. It's not good for you and it makes me nervous.' She stood there staring at me until I let my legs drop. 'That's better.' Scrape, scrape. Barry sang on, about New England.

I still wasn't sure what had brought me down from my bed so early on a Saturday, aside from the noise of my mother loosening icebergs from our Frigidaire. I hadn't slept well, with my dress for the wedding hanging from the curtain rod, fluttering in the white light of the street lamp outside my window. At 2 p.m. my father was marrying Lorna Queen, of 'Lorna Queen's Weather Scene' on WTSB News Channel 5. She was what they called a meteorologist and what my mother called the Weather Pet, but only when she was feeling vindictive. Lorna was blonde and perky and wore cute little pastel suits that showed just enough leg as she stood smiling in front of colourful maps, sweeping her arm as if she controlled all the elements. My father, Mac McPhail, was the sports anchor for Channel 5, and he and the Weather

Pet shared the subordinate news desk, away from the grim-faced anchors, Charlie Baker and Tess Phillips, who reported real news. Before we'd known about my father's affair with the Weather Pet, I'd always wondered what they were smiling and talking about in those last few minutes of the broadcast as the credits rolled. Charlie Baker and Tess Phillips shuffled important-looking papers, worn thin from a hard day of news chasing and news delivering, but my father and the Weather Pet were always off to the side sharing some secret laugh that the rest of us weren't in on. And when we finally did catch on it wasn't very funny after all.

Not that I didn't like Lorna Queen. She was nice enough for someone who broke up my parents' marriage. My mother, in all fairness, always blamed my father and limited her hostility to the nickname Weather Pet and to the occasional snide remark about my father's growing mass of hair, which at the time of the separation was receding with great speed and now seemed to have reversed itself and grown back with the perseverance and quickness of our lawn after a few good days of rain. My mother had read all the books about divorce and tried hard to make it smooth for me and my sister, Ashley, who was Daddy's pet and left the room at even the slightest remark about his hair. My mother kept her outbursts about that to a minimum, but I could tell by the way she winced when they showed my father and Lorna together at their subordinate news desk that it still hurt. Before the divorce my mother had been good at outbursts, and this quietness, this holding back, was more unnerving than I imagined any breakdown could be. My mother, like Ashley, has always cultivated the family dramatic streak, started by my grandmother, who at important family gatherings liked to fake horrible incidents if she felt she were not getting enough attention. No reunion, wedding or funeral was complete without at least one stroke, heart attack or general collapse from Grandma at which time everyone shifted into High Dramatic Mode, fussing and running around and generally creating the kind of chaos that my family is well known for.

This always made me kind of nervous. I hadn't inherited that flair for the stage that Ashley and my mother had, this snap ability to lose control in appropriate instances. I was more like my father, steady and worried all the time. Back then, we had it down to a science: Mom and Ashley overreacting, thriving on crisis, my father and I standing calm, together, balancing them out. Then my father left and, like a table short a leg, things had been out of whack ever since.

'So are you going?' That was Ashley, standing in the kitchen doorway in a T-shirt and socks. Just looking at her made me acutely aware of my own height, the pointedness of my elbows and hipbones, the extra inch I'd put on in the last month. At twenty-one my sister is a petite five-four, with the kind of curvy, rounded body that I wish I'd been born with;

tiny feet, perfect hair, small enough to be cute but still a force to be reckoned with. At my age she had already been voted Most Popular, dated (and dumped) the captain of the football team and been a varsity cheerleader. She was always the one at the top of the pyramid, tiny enough to be passed from hand to hand overhead until she stood high over everyone else, a bit shaky but triumphant, before letting loose and tumbling head over heels to be caught at the bottom with a sweep of someone's arms. I remembered her in her cheerleading uniform, short blue skirt, white sweater and saddle shoes, grabbing her backpack to run out to a carful of teenagers waiting outside, squealing off to school with a beep of the horn. Back then, Ashley seemed to live a life just like Barbie's: popular and perfect, always with a handsome boyfriend and the cool crowd. All she needed was the Dreamhouse and a purple plastic Corvette to make it real.

Now, my sister just scowled at me when she caught

me looking at her, then scratched one foot with the other. She had a good tan already, and on the inside of her left ankle I could see the yellow butterfly tattoo she'd got in Myrtle Beach when she'd got drunk after high-school graduation two years earlier and someone double dared her. Ashley was wild, but that was before she got engaged.

'No. I don't think I should go,' my mother said. 'I think it's in bad taste.'

'Go where?' I said.

'She invited you,' Ashley said, yawning. 'She wouldn't have done that if she didn't want you there.'

'Where?' I said again, but of course no one was listening to me. There was another crash as a block of ice fell out of the freezer.

'I'm not going,' my mother said solidly, planting a hand on her hip. 'It's tacky and I won't do it.'

'So don't do it,' Ashley said, coming into the kitchen and reaching across me to pick up a pack of frozen waffles from the table.

'Do what?' I said again, louder this time because in our house you have to make a commotion to even be heard.

'Go to your father's wedding,' my mother said. 'Lorna sent me an invitation.'

'She did?'

'Yes.' This fell into the category of whether Lorna, the Weather Pet, was either downright mean or just stupid. She did a lot of things that made me question this, from telling me it was okay to call her Mom once she married my father to sending my mother a framed picture of an old family Christmas card she'd found among my dad's junk. We'd all sat round the kitchen table, staring at it, my mother holding it in one hand with a puckered look on her face. She'd never said a word about it, but instead went outside and ripped up weeds in the garden for forty-five minutes, handful after handful flying over her head in a massive horticultural tantrum. I believed Lorna was mostly mean, bordering on stupid; my mother refused to even voice an opinion; and because Ashley couldn't bear to criticize anything about Daddy she said Lorna was just stupid and left mean out of it altogether. All I knew was that I would never call a woman only five years older than Ashley Mom and that that framed Christmas card was what Ann Landers would call In Quite Poor Taste.

So my mother was not with us as we set off for the church that afternoon, in our matching shiny pink bridesmaid dresses, to see our father be bonded in holy matrimony to this probably stupid but quite possibly just mean Weather Pet. I'd felt sorry for my mother as she lined us up in front of the mantel to take a picture with her little Instamatic, cooing about how lovely we looked. She stood in the doorway behind the screen, waving as we walked out to the car, the camera dangling from her wrist, and I realized suddenly why Ashley might have wanted her to come, even if it was tacky. There was something so sad about leaving her behind, all of a sudden, and

I had an urge to run back and take her with me, to pull that tether tight and hold her close. But I didn't, like I always don't, and instead climbed into the car next to Ashley and watched my mother waving as we pulled away from the house. At every wedding someone stays home.

As we got out of the car at the church, I saw Ashley's fiancé, Lewis Warsher, heading our way from the other end of the lot where he'd parked his little blue Chevette. He was fixing his tie as he walked, because Lewis was a neat dresser. He always wore shiny shoes and skinny ties in pastel colours. When Ashley saw him, I swear she shrank about two inches; there is something about Lewis that turns my sister, who is tough as nails, into a swooning, breathless belle.

'Hey, honey.' And of course they were immediately connected, his arms slipping round her small waist, pulling her close for one of those long, emotional hugs where it looked like he was the only thing that was keeping her from collapsing to the ground. Ashley and Lewis spent a lot of time hugging each other, supporting each other physically and whispering. They gave me a complex, always with their heads together murmuring in corners of rooms, their voices too low to catch anything but a few vowels.

'Hey,' Ashley whispered. They were still hugging. I stood there fiddling with my dress; I had no choice but to wait. Ashley hadn't always been this way; she'd had boyfriends for as long as I could remember, but none of them had affected her like Lewis. For years we kept track of major family events by whom Ashley had been dating at the time. During the Mitchell period, I got my braces and Grandma came to live with us. The Robert era included my mother going back to night school and Ashley getting in the car wreck that broke her leg and made her get the stitches that left a heart-shaped scar on her right shoulder. And it was during the year-long Frank ordeal that the divorce came down, complete with law proceedings, family therapy and the advent of Lorna, the Weather Pet. It was a boyfriend timeline: I could not remember dates, but I could place each important event in my life with a face of a boy whose heart Ashley had broken.

But this was all before Lewis, whom Ashley met at the Yoghurt Paradise at the mall where they both worked. Ashley was a Vive cosmetics salesgirl, which meant she stood behind a big counter in Dillard's department store, wearing a white lab coat and putting overpriced make-up on rich ladies' faces. She thought she was something in that lab coat, wearing it practically everywhere like it meant she was a damn doctor or something. She was just coming out of the messy break-up of the Frank era and was consoling herself with a yoghurt sundae when Lewis Warsher sensed her pain and sat himself down at her table because she looked like she needed a friend. These are their words, which I know because I've heard this story entirely too many times since they announced their engagement six months ago.

My mother said Ashley missed our father, and needed a protective figure; Lewis just came along at the right time. And Lewis *did* protect her, from old boyfriends and petrol-station attendants and bugs that dared to cross her path. Still, sometimes I wondered what she really saw in him. There was nothing spectacular about Lewis, and it was a little unsettling to see my sister, whom I'd always admired for being plucky and tough and not taking a bit of lip from anyone, shrinking into his arms whenever the world rose up to meet her face to face.

'Hey, Haven.' Lewis leaned over and pecked me on the cheek, still holding Ashley close. 'You look beautiful.'

'Thanks,' I said. Lewis had the arm clamp on Ashley, steering her towards the church, with me following. Even though we were wearing the same god-awful pink fluffy dresses, we looked totally different. Ashley was a short, curvy pink rose, and I was a tall, pink straw, like something you'd plonk down in a big fizzy drink. This was the kind of thing I was always thinking about since my body had betrayed me and made me a giant.

When I was in first grade, I had a teacher named Mrs Thomas. She was young, sported a flip hairdo that made her look just like Snow White, smelled like Lily of the Valley and kept a picture of a man in a uniform on her desk, staring stiffly out from the frame. And even though I was shy and slow at maths she didn't care. She loved me. She'd come up beside me in the lunch line or during story hour and smooth her hand over my head, saying, 'Why, Miss Haven, you're just no bigger than a minute.' I was compact at six, able to fit neatly into small places that now were inaccessible: under the crook of an arm, in the palm of a hand. At five eleven and counting, I no longer had the sense that someone like Mrs Thomas could neatly enclose me if danger should strike. I was all bony elbows and acute angles, like a jigsaw puzzle piece that can only go in the middle, waiting for the others to fit around it to make it whole.

The church was filling up with people, which wasn't surprising: my father is the kind of person who knows everybody somehow. Mac McPhail, sportscaster, beer drinker, teller of tall tales and big lies, the latter being told mostly to my mother in the last few months of the marriage. I can remember sitting in front of the TV watching my father on the local news every night, seeing the sly sideways looks he and Lorna Queen exchanged during the leads into commercial breaks, and still not having any idea that he would leave my mother for this woman best known for her short skirts and pouty-lipped way of saying 'upper-level disturbance'. She didn't know the half of it. There had been no disturbance before like the one that hit our house the day my father came home from the station, sat my mother down at the kitchen table right under the vent that leads to the floor beneath the counter in my bathroom and dropped the bomb that he'd fallen hard for the Weather Pet. I sat on the side of the bath, toothbrush in hand, and wished the house had been designed differently so I wouldn't have been privy to this most painful of moments. My mother was silent for a long time, my father's voice the only one wafting up through the floor, explaining how he couldn't help it, didn't want to lie any more, had to come clean, all of this with his booming sportscaster voice, so agile at curving round scores and highlights, stumbling over the simple truth that his marriage was over. My mother started crying, finally, and then told him to leave in a quiet, steady voice that made the room seem suddenly colder. Two weeks later he had moved into the Weather Pet's condo. He met me and Ashley for lunch each Saturday and took us to the beach every other weekend, spending too much money and trying to explain everything by putting his arm round my shoulder, squeezing, and sighing aloud.

But that had been a year and a half ago, and now here it was wedding day, the *first* wedding I was dreading this summer. We walked into the lobby of the church and were immediately gathered up in the large arms of my aunt Ree, who was representing the bulk of my father's side of the family, most of whom were still upset about the divorce and sided with my mother, family loyalty notwithstanding. But Aunt Ree was ample enough to represent everyone in her flowing pink muumuu, a corsage the size of a small bush pinned to her chest.

'Haven, you come over here and give your aunt Ree some sugar.' She squashed me against her, and I could feel the flowers poking into my skin. She'd clamped Ashley in her other arm, somehow getting her away from Lewis, and hugged us both as tightly together as if she were trying to consolidate us into one person. 'And, Ashley, this should all seem pretty familiar to you. When's your big day again?'

'August nineteenth,' Lewis said quickly. I wondered

if that was the answer he gave to any question now. It was what I usually said.

Aunt Ree pushed me back, holding me by both arms as Ashley made a quick dash back to Lewis. 'Now you are just growing like a weed, I swear to God. Look at you. How tall are you?'

I smiled, fighting the urge to slouch. 'Too tall.'

'No such thing.' She tightened her grip on my arm. 'You can never be too tall or too thin. That's what they say, isn't it?'

'It's too rich or too thin.' Ashley said. Leave it to my short, curvy sister to correct even a misworded compliment.

'Whatever,' Aunt Ree said. 'You're beautiful, anyway. But we're running late and the bride is a mess. We've got to go find you your bouquets.'

Ashley kissed Lewis and clung to him for a few more seconds before following me and Aunt Ree through the masses of perfumed wedding guests to a side door that led into a big room with bookcases covering all four walls. Lorna Queen was sitting at a table in the corner, a make-up mirror facing her, with some woman hovering around picking at her hair with a long comb.

'We're here!' Aunt Ree said in a singsong voice, presenting us in all of our pink as if she'd created us herself. 'And just in time.'

Lorna Queen *was* a beautiful woman. As she turned in her seat to face us, I realized that again, just as I always did when I watched her doing her forecasts in her short skirts with colour-coordinated lipsticks. She was pert and perfect and had the tiniest little ears I'd ever seen on anyone. She kept them covered most of the time, but once at the beach I'd seen her with her hair pulled back, with those ears like seashells moulded against her skin. I'd always wondered if she heard like the rest of us or if the world sounded different through such small receptors.

'Hi, girls.' She smiled at us and dabbed her eyes with a neatly folded Kleenex. 'Y'all look beautiful.'

'Are you okay?' Ashley asked her.

'I'm fine. I'm just' – she sniffled daintily – 'so happy. I've waited for this day for so long, and I'm just so happy.'

The woman doing her make-up rolled her eyes. 'Lorna, honey, waterproof mascara can only do so much. You've got to stop crying.'

'I know.' She sniffled again, reaching out to take my hand and Ashley's. 'I want you girls to know how much I love your father. I'm going to make him just as happy as I can, and I'm so glad we're all going to be a family.'

'We're very happy for you,' Ashley said, speaking for both of us, which she often did when Lorna was concerned.

Lorna was tearing up again when a man in a suit came in through another door and whispered, 'Ten minutes,' then flashed the thumbs-up sign as if we were about to go out and play the Big Game.

'Ten minutes,' Lorna said, her hand fluttering out

of mine and to her face, dabbing her eyes. The make-up woman spun her back round in the chair and moved in with the powder puff. 'My God, it's actually happening.'

Ashley reached into her bag and pulled out a lipstick. 'Do like this,' she said to me, pursing her lips. I did, and she put some on me, smoothing it across with a finger. 'It's not really your colour, but it'll do.'

I stood there while she added some more eye shadow and blush to my face, all the while looking at me through half-shut eyes, practising her craft, her face very close to mine. This was the Ashley I remembered from my childhood, when the five-year gap didn't seem that large and we set up our Barbie worlds in the driveway every day after school, my Ken fraternizing with her Skipper. This was the Ashley who painted my nails at the kitchen table during long summers, the back door swinging in the breeze and the radio on. This was the Ashley who came into my room late one night after breaking up with Robert Losard and sat on the edge of my bed crying until I wrapped my arms awkwardly round her and smoothed her hair, trying to understand the words she was saying. This was the Ashley who had climbed out on the roof with me all those nights in the first few months of the divorce and told me how much she missed my father. This was the Ashley I loved, away from Lewis's clinging hands and the wedding plans and the five-year-wide impasse that neither of us could cross.

'There.' She capped the lipstick and dumped all the make-up back in her bag. 'Now just don't cry too much and you'll be fine.'

'I won't cry,' I said, and suddenly aware of Lorna looking at us behind her in the mirror I added, 'I never cry at weddings.'

'Oh, I do,' Lorna said. 'There's something about a wedding, something so perfect and so sad, all at the same time. I bawl at weddings.'

'You better not be bawling out there.' The make-up lady dabbed with the powder puff. 'If this stuff doesn't hold up, you'll look a mess.'

The door opened and a woman in a dress the same shade as ours but without the long flowing skirt came in, carrying a big box of flowers. 'Helen!' Lorna said, tearing up again. 'You look lovely.'

Helen was obviously Lorna's sister, seeing as how she also had those tiny little seashell ears. I figured it had to be more than coincidence. They hugged and Helen turned towards us, clasping her hands together. 'This must be Ashley and Haven. Lorna said you were tall.' She leaned forward and kissed my cheek, then Ashley's. 'And I hear congratulations are in order for you. When's the big day?'

'August nineteenth,' Ashley said. It was the million-dollar question.

'My, that's soon! Are you getting nervous?'

'No, not really,' Ashley said. 'I'm just ready to get it all over with.'

'Amen to that,' Lorna said, standing up and removing the paper bib from round her neck. She took a deep breath, holding her palm against her stomach. 'I swear I have never been so nervous, even when I did that marathon at the station during the hurricane. Do I look all right?'

'You look lovely,' Helen said. We all nodded in agreement. An older woman appeared, gesturing frantically. Her lips were moving as if long, un-pronounceable words were coming out, but I couldn't hear a thing she was saying. As she came closer, I made out something that sounded like, 'It's time, it's time,' but she was warbling so it could have been anything.

'Okay,' the Weather Pet said with one last sniff. Ashley checked my face again, licking her lips and telling me to do the same and with Lorna Queen behind us, her sister Helen carrying her train, we proceeded to the lobby of the church.

We'd practised all this the night before, when I'd

been wearing shorts and sandals and the aisle seemed like a hop, skip and jump to the spot where the minister had been standing in blue jeans and a T-shirt that said Clean and Free Baptist Retreat. Now the church was packed and the aisle seemed about a hundred miles long with the minister standing at the end of it like a tiny plastic figure you might slap on to a cake. We got pushed into figuration, with me of course behind Ashley since I was taller and then Helen and then Lorna, who was telling us all how much she loved us. Finally the mad whisperer walked right to the front of the line, waved her arm wildly like she was flagging a plane in to land right there in the middle of the church, and we were on our way.

The night before, they'd said to count to seven after Ashley left, so I gave it eight because I was nervous and then took my first step. I felt like the man on stilts in the circus who walks as if the wind is blowing him sideways. I tried not to look at anything but the middle of Ashley's back, which was not altogether interesting but somewhat better than all the faces staring back at me. As I got closer to the minister, I got the nerve to look up and see my father, who was standing next to his best friend, Rick Bickman, smiling.

My father only does one impression, but it's a good one. He can do a perfect rendition of the munchkin who greets Dorothy right after she lands on the witch in the *Wizard of Oz*, the one who with two others sings that silly song about being the Lollipop Guild. They rock back and forth and their faces get all contorted. My father only does this when he's drunk or when a bunch of what my mother calls his bad-seed friends are around; but suddenly it was all I could think of, as if at any moment he might forget all this nonsense and start singing that damn song.

It didn't happen, of course, because this was a wedding and serious business. Instead my father winked at me as I took my place next to Ashley and we all turned and faced the direction we'd come and waited for Lorna Queen to make her entrance.

There was a pause in the music, long enough for me to take a quick glance around to see if I recognized anyone, which I didn't because all I could see was the backs of everyone's heads as they waited for Lorna to appear. Charlie Baker, Important Local News Anchor, was giving her away. There had been a long story in the paper this very morning about the novelty wedding of the sports guy and the weather girl, which went into detail about the mentoring relationship between Charlie Baker and the intern he'd taken under his wing during her first shaky days at the station. My mother had left the article out on the kitchen table, without comment, and as I scanned I realized it could have been about strangers for all the attachment I felt to my father's fairy-tale second marriage.

Lorna was beaming as she came down the aisle.

Her eyes sparkled and the waterproof mascara wasn't holding up the way it should have but no matter – she was still beautiful. When she and Charlie got up to the front she leaned forward and kissed Helen, then Ashley and then me, her veil scratching my face as it brushed against me. It was the first time I'd seen Charlie Baker, anchorman, close up, and I would have bet money he'd had a facelift sometime during those long news-doing years. He had that slippery look to him.

The minister cleared his throat, Charlie Baker handed Lorna over to my father and now, finally, it was really happening. Some woman in the front row, wearing a purple hat, started crying immediately, and as the minister got to the vows Helen was tearing up as well. I was bored and kept glancing around the church, wondering what my mother would think of all this, a fancy church and a long walk down the aisle, pomp and circumstance. My parents were married in the Party Room of the Dominic Hotel in Atlantic City, with only her mother and his parents in attendance, along with a few lost partygoers who stumbled in from a bar mitzvah a couple of doors down. It was low-key, just what they needed, seeing that my mother's father disapproved and refused to attend and my father's family couldn't afford much more than the Party Room for a couple of hours, a cake and a cousin playing the piano; my father had paid for the justice of the peace. There are pictures of them all around one table together, my mother and father and grandmother and my father's parents, plus some white-haired man in Buddy Holly glasses, each of them with a plate of half-eaten cake before them. This was the wedding party.

I watched my father, thinking this as he said his vows, speaking evenly into Lorna's veil with his face very red and serious. My sister began to cry and I knew it wasn't for the happiness of weddings but for the finality of all of this, knowing that things would never go back to the way they were. I thought of my mother at home in her garden, weeding under a hot afternoon sun, away from the pealing of church bells. And I thought of other summers, long before my father lifted this veil and kissed his new bride.

Look out for
Just Listen

I'm Annabel.
I'm the girl who has it all.
Model looks, confidence, a great
social life. I'm one of the lucky ones.
Aren't I?

My 'best friend' is spreading rumours about me.
My family is slowly falling apart. It's turning into a long, lonely
summer, full of secrets and silence.

But I've met this guy who won't let me hide away.
He's one of those intense types, obsessed with music.
He's determined to make me listen.

And he's determined to make me smile.
But can he help me forget
what happened the night
everything changed?

Don't Miss

Just Listen and
The Truth about Forever

'I feel everything your characters feel, it's incredible. No other author can do that to me' – *Brandi*, MySpace user

'I don't know how to explain how amazing your books are' – MySpace user

'Unputdownable' – *Mizz*

'Beautifully structured and profound' – *The Observer*

Fiction to fall in love with from bestselling, award-winning author **Sarah Dessen**.

Meet
Sarah Dessen

Did you always want to be a writer?

As far back as I remember, I've been writing. I've always had this wild imagination, and I love to embellish stories to make them more interesting. When I left school I wrote like crazy. At times it seemed stupid – I was broke and there was no guarantee that anything would come of it. Luckily, it did. But even if I hadn't sold a book I'd still be writing. It becomes part of you, just something you do.

Who were your favourite authors as a child and who are you into now?

I really liked Judy Blume and Lois Lowry. Currently I'm really into Anne Tyler, who wrote *The Accidental Tourist*. John Irving's *A Prayer for Owen Meany* is probably my favourite book right now.

What was your favourite subject at school?

English. Anything to do with writing and reading. I'd been writing forever, but I got frustrated in school because there were rules about what you were Supposed To Write. I wanted to be able to make everything up, even then.

Where do you get your ideas?

This is a hard question, and there's no single answer. Usually I start with something that did happen to me or to someone I know, and build on it from there. There are so many stories out there waiting to be told. You just have to keep your eyes open.

What's your best advice for aspiring writers?

I think, first of all, you have to believe in yourself and your work. Writing can be really solitary, so you have to be not only your own harshest critic but also your own biggest fan. But what really matters above all is that you are writing. When I'm working on a book I'm at the computer every day. Work out what time of day you get your best work done, and try to write at that same time, every day.

Bright and shiny and sizzling with fun stuff . . .

puffin.co.uk

WEB FUN

UNIQUE and exclusive digital content!
Podcasts, photos, Q&A, Day in the Life of, interviews and much more, from Eoin Colfer, Cathy Cassidy, Allan Ahlberg and Meg Rosoff to Lynley Dodd!

WEB NEWS

The **Puffin Blog** is packed with posts and photos from Puffin HQ and special guest bloggers. You can also sign up to our monthly newsletter **Puffin Beak Speak**

WEB CHAT

Discover something new EVERY month – books, competitions and treats galore

WEBBED FEET

(Puffins have funny little feet and brightly coloured beaks)

Point your mouse our way today!

It all started with a Scarecrow.

Puffin is seventy years old.
Sounds ancient, doesn't it? But Puffin has never been
so lively. We're always on the lookout for the next big
idea, which is how it began all those years ago.

Penguin Books was a big idea from the mind of
a man called Allen Lane, who in 1935 invented
the quality paperback and changed the world.
**And from great Penguins, great Puffins grew,
changing the face of children's books forever.**

The first four Puffin Picture Books were hatched in 1940 and the
first Puffin story book featured a man with broomstick arms called
Worzel Gummidge. In 1967 Kaye Webb, Puffin Editor, started the
Puffin Club, promising to **'make children into readers'**.
She kept that promise and over 200,000 children became
devoted Puffineers through their quarterly instalments of
Puffin Post, which is now back for a new generation.

Many years from now, we hope you'll look back and
remember Puffin with a smile. **No matter what your age
or what you're into, there's a Puffin for everyone.**
The possibilities are endless, but one thing is for sure:
whether it's a picture book or a paperback, a sticker book
or a hardback, **if it's got that little Puffin
on it – it's bound to be good.**